Stella in the Vila

Andrea F Nunes

Claudia Emanuele Bernardino

ISBN: 978-0-578-79052-7

By: *Andrea F Nunes*
Illustrated by: *Claudia Emanuele Bernardino*

Published in the United States of America.

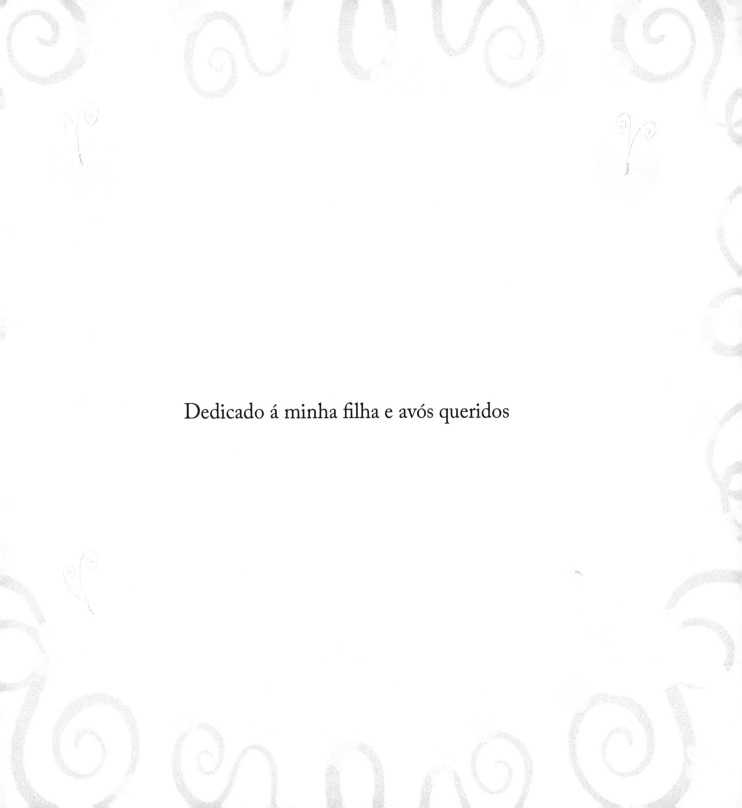

Dedicado á minha filha e avós queridos

"Good morning, Avó and Avô!"
"Bom dia, meu amor", they say.
Let's have some eggs for breakfast
and go have a great big day!

To start our day let's check the coop
for **ovos** the chickens laid.
We'll find them in their hiding spots
and be proud of what they've made!

Now let's see the **coelhos**
and go feed them some **alface**.
They love it when we pet them,
their big ears are oh so soft!

It's time to do some gardening
over there in our **jardim**.
We'll water all the flowers
and then have some good **pudim!**

"são horas de almoçar!"
Avô has come home from hard work.
Let's set the table nice and neat,
and serve what we have cooked!

We have some yummy **sopa**,
Avó makes the very best.
She uses lots of veggies
that she grew and then she blessed.

The afternoon is sunny
and it gets a little hot.
Let's sit here in the **sombra**
where we like to sit a lot.

It's time to visit **primos**
and our aunts and uncles too.
On our walk we see the sheep
and hear the cows go moo.

It's always fun to walk around,
this town has lots of charm...
Like up by the **igreja**
or back down by grandpa's farm.

We walk through the big **festa**
in the middle of the town.
We love to dance around the square
and **bato pé** around!

The **sol** is starting to get dim.
It's time to go back home.
I'll put my hand in your hand
so we don't walk home alone.

queijo and **pão** for dinner,
Wow, that's just my favorite treat!
A **pastel de nata** on the side,
A meal that can't be beat!

It's **banho** time to prep for bed
and put my PJs on.
I slip on my **pantufas,**
it feels like my own salon!

I love to cuddle my **avós,**
they're just the best there are.
I love them with my whole heart,
even more so when we're far.

«É hora de dormir!»
It's time to get tucked in.
Vó gives me a big **beijo,**
what a great big day it's been!

Although we might live very far,
across an ocean wide,
far enough to take a plane
for an 8 hour ride...

The love we have is so strong,
it's beyond any **valor**.
We love each other so, so much,
I am their **«meu amor»**.

Printed in the USA
CPSIA information can be obtained
at www.ICGtesting.com
LVHW070822240823
755848LV00054B/776